Inspector Chopra and the Million-Dollar Motor Car

Vaseem Khan

MULHOLLAND
BOOKS

HODDER

First published in Great Britain in 2018 by Mulholland Books
An imprint of Hodder & Stoughton
An Hachette UK company

1

A CIP catalogue record for this title is available from the British Library

Paperback ISBN 978 1 473 65015 2
eBook ISBN 978 1 473 65016 9

Typeset in ITC Stone Serif Std by Palimpsest Book Production Limited,
Falkirk, Stirlingshire
Printed and bound by CPI Group (UK) Ltd, Croydon, CR0 4YY

Hodder & Stoughton policy is to use papers that are natural,
renewable and recyclable products and made from wood grown in
sustainable forests. The logging and manufacturing processes are
expected to conform to the environmental regulations of the
country of origin.

Hodder & Stoughton Ltd
Carmelite House
50 Victoria Embankment
London EC4Y 0DZ

www.hodder.co.uk

To all those who have always found reading a challenge . . . Don't give up. Never give up, because we will never give up writing stories for you to read.

The Missing Mercedes

'That van needs a new paint job.'

Inspector Ashwin Chopra (Retired) turned to see a middle-aged white man walking towards him along the busy, smog-filled road.

It was a typical March morning in the Indian city of Mumbai. The air was hot enough to burn your lungs. The road was a hell of honking rickshaws, hooting trucks, roaring motorbikes and belching cars. A stream of people flowed along both sides of the street. Cows, goats, donkeys and stray dogs added to the chaos.

Chopra had parked his van in front of his restaurant which was called Poppy's.

He had opened Poppy's when he had had to retire from the police due to a heart problem.

Poppy's was named after his wife, and also served as the office for the Baby Ganesh Detective Agency. The agency allowed Chopra to carry on using the skills he had gained over a thirty-year career. Even though he no longer wore a uniform, justice was still very important to him.

Chopra watched as the white man came nearer. The man had short brown hair with streaks of grey, a hard jaw and bright blue eyes. He stuck out a hand. 'My name is Carter. Jon Carter,' he said, in an English accent.

'Chopra,' said Chopra.

'I know who you are,' said Carter. 'I saw your picture in the paper.'

The year before, Chopra had stopped a major crime ring in the city. This had led him to open his detective agency, and it had got his name and photograph in lots of newspapers.

'I need your help,' said Carter.

'Give me a second.' Chopra went to the rear of the van, let down the ramp and waited as Ganesha trotted down into the road.

Ganesha was the one-year-old baby elephant sent to Chopra by his long-lost Uncle Bansi. Bansi had not explained why he was sending him the animal. But he had also sent a letter saying, 'This is no ordinary elephant'.

At first Chopra had not known what to do with the strange gift. But in time Ganesha had become a part of his and Poppy's lives. The little elephant was very bright, and adored by everyone. Now he even went with Chopra on cases around the city.

In a sense, Ganesha was Chopra's 'partner',

though he would never say that out loud to anyone.

Chopra settled the elephant calf under the mango tree in the yard behind the restaurant. Then he led Carter to his office.

He ordered two fresh lime juices, then waited for the Englishman to explain.

'Have you heard of the Premier No.1 Deluxe Car dealership and garage?' asked Carter.

Chopra nodded.

Everyone knew about Premier No.1.

It had opened with great fanfare in Mumbai some years ago, the first luxury car importer in the city. Mumbai was the richest city in India and it showed on the streets. Company bosses, movie stars, famous sportsmen and women – everyone in the city wanted to drive the best car they could afford. So sales of such cars had rocketed with all the new money that had flowed into the country. And for the best cars of all there was only one place to go: Premier No.1.

Of course, thought Chopra darkly, as in most places around the world, while the rich got richer, the poor just got poorer. There were no luxury cars for the ordinary man on the street in India. They made do with rickshaws, taxis, broken-down buses, crowded trains and the humble bicycle.

'I am the general manager at Premier No.1,' said Carter. 'I sell luxury cars for a living. You want a Ferrari? No problem. Lamborghini, easy peasy, I can even throw in the fluffy dice. There's no car we can't get. That is why everyone comes to us . . .

'Well, a month ago we got a special order. The priciest car we have ever sold. A 1954 Mercedes-Benz Formula 1 racing car, the same car that world champion Juan Manuel Fangio drove. We bought the car for our client, and he then asked us to upgrade it. New seats, paint job, the works.' Carter paused. 'Yesterday the car vanished from our garage.'

'Vanished?' echoed Chopra.

'Vanished,' said Carter grimly, nodding. 'A car worth four million dollars. Gone!'

Chopra was amazed. How could any car be worth four million dollars? It was hard to believe. People were starving every day in his country and someone was paying four million for an old car! 'So why have you come to me?' he said. 'Why not tell the police?'

'We can't,' said Carter. 'This car is a present for our client's son. His twenty-first birthday is tomorrow, and he's a big motor racing fan. His dad gives him anything he wants. And this dad

4

is a man named Bobby Jindal. I guess you have heard of him?'

Chopra nodded.

Everyone had heard of Bobby Jindal.

Bobby Jindal was a dark figure from Mumbai's underworld, a man known for violence. He had built up a criminal empire, and had then gone into property and other legal businesses.

He was feared by everyone: his rivals, ordinary people and even the police.

'If Jindal finds out, it will be awful,' said Carter. 'My boss, Dinshaw, wants you to find the car in the next twenty-four hours. If you don't we are both dead men. Like I said, I am the garage's general manager. At the end of the day, it's my fault.' Carter's eyes burned into Chopra. 'I have a family. You must help me!'

The Premier No. 1 Deluxe Car Garage

The Premier No.1 garage was in the rich Mumbai suburb of Bandra.

Chopra drove his van through the front gates and parked.

He followed the manager, Jon Carter, into the garage.

Inside, he saw rows and rows of cars, vans, trucks and motorbikes. He saw Ferraris, Porsches, Mercedes, BMWs and Jaguars. There was even a tractor painted gold. Staff moved between the rows, dressed in red uniforms. In the corner, cars moved through a giant car wash.

Ganesha, padding along behind Chopra, flapped his ears as he spotted the car wash. The giant machine had grabbed his attention right away.

'Where was the Mercedes parked?' asked Chopra.

Carter showed him to a bay marked 53. There were cars on either side, a Bentley and a Range Rover. In front there was a row of gleaming motorbikes, and behind there were three dark vans.

There was nothing to see in the bay. Just an empty space.

'We finished work on the Mercedes last night,' said Carter. 'I'm due to send the car to Bobby Jindal tomorrow.' He barked at a mechanic, who rushed away and returned holding a plastic wallet. Inside the wallet was a small black card. Carter handed it to Chopra. 'We found this on the floor in the empty bay.'

Chopra studied the card. It said, in Hindi:

A trickster came, and this was seen,
In a cage went a parrot that was green,
How amazing is what everybody said,
What went in green, came out red!

'My staff tell me it's some sort of riddle,' said Carter. 'I can't read Hindi myself.'

'They are correct,' said Chopra. He read out the riddle, in English, for Carter. 'But I don't know what it means,' he said.

'Hmm,' said Carter, looking thoughtful. 'The only thing I can think of is that the Mercedes used to be green. Now, after the paint job, it is red. But I don't know what a parrot has to do with it.'

7

There was a sudden fuss.

Chopra turned to see a gang of mechanics around the entrance to the car wash. They were waving their arms, and shouting.

'Your elephant!' called one. 'He's gone in the wash.'

Chopra raced to the car wash.

He looked in, but all he could see was the back of a Bentley passing between two rollers.

'Come on,' said Carter, and led Chopra to the far end.

They waited anxiously. A black BMW 5 series emerged and then, behind it, came Ganesha. The drying fan ruffled the short hairs on the top of his head. He flapped his ears happily as Chopra scolded him.

He checked the little elephant was all right.

Then he asked Carter about the security at the garage.

'There were three guards on the front gate. As for the garage itself, a steel shutter rolls down when we close up. That was locked. We also have CCTV but it doesn't show a thing.'

'What about the back?'

'There's only a steel fire door that lets on to an alley. But you can't get a car through that. Besides, it was locked.'

'Show me.'

Carter led Chopra through the garage's back offices and a kitchen to the rear door.

He opened it and they went into an alley with high walls on both sides. Sunlight shone down into the alley. There was a tall iron gate at the far end of the alley, with coils of barbed wire on top.

'That was locked too,' said Carter. He sighed. 'There's just no way anyone could have got into and out of this garage without us knowing. Let alone make a car vanish into thin air. Some of the men are saying it's magic,' he added.

'But you don't believe that,' said Chopra.

'I am a practical man,' said Carter. 'I know that many Indians believe in magic and all that mumbo-jumbo, but not me.'

'How many people work here?'

'We have twenty-two staff. Why? Do you think it was an inside job?'

'It usually is.'

Carter shook his head. 'I *have* thought about that, of course. But I know these people. I trust them. It can't be one of them.'

'I wouldn't be so sure,' said Chopra. During his thirty years in the police, he had learned that complete trust was a rare thing. He had another idea. 'Don't your cars have GPS trackers?'

'Not unless the client asks for them. This is a classic car. It would be a crime to fit it with modern kit.'

Carter's mobile phone rang. He turned away to answer it.

Chopra noticed Ganesha snuffling around behind the door. He was running his trunk down the dry sewer along the alley wall. An elephant's trunk is one of the most sensitive organs in the animal kingdom. Ganesha was always finding things that Chopra had missed. He had often thought that having Ganesha was better than having his own forensics team.

He watched as the little elephant picked up something with the tip of his trunk. 'What have you got there, boy?'

Ganesha held up his trunk.

Chopra took the object and looked at it.

It was a small brown bottle. Inside were pills. There was no name on the bottle, just the name of the pills, on a white label.

It could just be rubbish, Chopra thought. But then again, it might be important. And the alley had been swept clean. Whoever had dropped this must have done so not long ago.

He put the bottle in his pocket.

Carter had finished his phone call.

'I need to speak to your staff,' said Chopra.

Chopra spent the next two hours talking to the staff at the garage.

It wasn't until he spoke to the garage's accountant, a plump middle-aged lady in glasses, that he learned something useful. The woman, Maria Nova, suddenly burst into tears. 'It wasn't my fault, sir,' she wailed.

Carter looked at the woman, amazed. 'Did you have something to do with this, Maria?'

Chopra offered the woman a hanky. 'No, sir,' said Maria, dabbing at her eyes.

'Then why are you crying?' asked Carter.

'Because I think I know who did it.'

'Who?' asked Carter, leaning forward.

'Mr Felix.'

'Who is Mr Felix?' asked Chopra.

'Felix Pinto,' said Carter. 'Our head mechanic. Come to think of it, where is he today?'

'That's the problem,' said Maria sadly. 'He has told everyone he is with a parts supplier.'

'But that's not where he is, is it, Maria?' said Chopra gently.

'No,' said Maria. 'He's at the racecourse. Again.'

A gambler never learns

Chopra drove to the Mahalaxmi racecourse, half an hour away in midtown Mumbai.

The racecourse was the most famous in India. It was run by the Royal Western India Turf Club, and it was where the Indian Derby took place each year.

The drive was a difficult one.

There was heavy traffic and the van's air conditioner struggled in the baking heat. The journey was further delayed when a man who was moving washing machines by handcart spilled them into the road. The chaos that followed almost caused a riot.

Eventually Chopra got to the racecourse. He parked his van and went inside. Ganesha trotted behind him.

Chopra had a picture of the head mechanic, Felix Pinto, with him. He used the picture to search for him. The crowd was quite small. This was a weekday and the race was a minor one.

Chopra looked around through his binoculars. He saw that some people were lined up next to the track. Only a short white fence lay between them and the racing turf.

In the starting stalls, jockeys got their horses ready for the race. They wore colourful silks, and were watched by bored-looking stewards.

And then Chopra saw a man wearing the uniform of the Premier No.1 garage.

Maria Nova, the garage accountant, had said that Felix Pinto had a serious gambling problem. She knew this because the pair of them were having an affair. Pinto was married, but Maria was not. Pinto had seduced the poor woman and had been borrowing money from her. He had even been asking her to take funds from the garage. Maria knew that Felix's gambling was out of control. She thought that he had stolen the Mercedes to fund his gambling habit.

Chopra moved towards the mechanic. He called out: 'Felix Pinto!'

Pinto turned around, and saw Chopra.

His round face, with its bouncy little moustache, looked around in panic.

Then he turned and jumped over the white fence and on to the track. He tripped up and fell in a heap on the grass.

'Stop!' said Chopra.

The race had started and the horses were

galloping around the track. Soon they would turn the corner and flatten Pinto. He was in real danger of being hurt.

Suddenly, a grey blur shot past Chopra.

Ganesha charged through the fence and on to the track. He wrapped his trunk around Pinto's ankle and hauled the little man backwards, just as the speeding horses arrived.

The thunder of hooves passed by Pinto's ears. Clods of earth landed on his head.

He got to his feet, shaking, and faced Chopra. 'Your elephant saved my life,' he said in wonder.

Chopra glared at him. 'Why did you run in the first place? I only wanted to talk to you.'

'I thought you were a gangster,' said Felix. 'I owe a lot of money to the wrong sort of people.'

Chopra gaped at the man. 'Since when do gangsters go around scaring people with baby elephants?' he asked.

'You are right. They don't. Why did you want to talk to me, anyway?'

Chopra told him the reason. Pinto's shoulders slumped. 'So the secret is out,' he said. 'Now everyone knows about my gambling problem. Carter will sack me for sure.'

Chopra said nothing.

'Well, sacking me won't get that car back,' said Pinto. 'Because I didn't take it. I was nowhere near the garage last night. After I left work, I was at my mother-in-law's house in south Mumbai, fixing her car. The old hag nagged me all night. I didn't get back to the garage until this morning.'

Chopra felt the man was telling the truth. It was, after all, an easy alibi to check. And besides, if Pinto's mother-in-law was like his own, she wouldn't spit on the pavement to help her son-in-law, let alone lie for him.

'If you ask my opinion, you're looking in the wrong place,' said Pinto.

'Where is the right place?'

'Veena Yash,' said Pinto. 'She used to work in our sales team. She was sacked three months ago. Made a big scene before she left. Swore she'd get her revenge.'

'And where can I find this Veena Yash?'

'Last I heard, she'd opened up some sort of estate agency in Juhu.'

Get in at the ground floor!

Juhu was another rich suburb of the city, a place that Bollywood movie stars and famous cricket players called home.

Chopra quickly found the Boom Time Property Agency on Juhu Tara Road, just a few doors down from the Marriott Hotel. On one side was a Barista coffee bar, on the other a Gucci store. This was the face of modern India.

Big brands and non-stop shopping.

But just a short walk away was a slum where whole families lived in tiny rooms. Kids were begging on the street just to survive. The thought made Chopra unhappy. He always felt unhappy when he thought about how unfair life could be in his country.

He walked through the front doors of Boom Time. He found himself in a vast showroom with a wooden floor that clacked loudly under Ganesha's feet. In the centre of the room was a plastic model of a new housing project. It was full of high-rise flats, swimming pools and fancy gardens. Along the sides of the room were life-sized mock-up bedrooms and bathrooms. Well-off couples were being shown around by smartly dressed salesmen and women.

Chopra listened for a moment to the sales pitch. It was all about rising prices, safe investments and upgrading your lifestyle.

When had a home stopped being just a home? he thought.

'It's superb, isn't it?'

Chopra turned to see a grinning young salesman with slicked-back hair marching towards him. 'It's the finest project in the city,' he said proudly. 'And right now is the best time to invest. Get in at the beginning – on the ground floor, if you'll pardon the pun!' He laughed, a loud, grating sound. It set Chopra's teeth on edge and made Ganesha hide behind him.

Heh! Heh! Heh!

The man spotted Ganesha. He stopped laughing. It was as if someone had pulled out his plug. 'Is that your elephant? I guess you will need a big bungalow then, with a garden and a cage?'

'He does not live in a cage,' Chopra growled.

'Elephants are dangerous,' said the man as if he were an expert. 'One day it's all cuddles and tricks, the next it's a mad elephant stamping on your head.'

Chopra was about to shout at the grinning idiot when he saw a woman approaching them. The woman was tall, dusky and very pretty. She was dressed in a skirt suit. 'How may we help you?' she asked, shooing away the young salesman.

She gave Chopra a smile like the sun shining on him.

'I am looking for Veena Yash,' said Chopra.

'You have found her,' said Yash. 'How may I help you?'

'A car has gone missing from Premier No.1. A very expensive car.'

Yash's smile vanished. Chopra felt as if someone had turned off the sun.

'And you came here to accuse *me*?' she said. 'You have a lot of nerve.'

'I was told you have a grudge against Dinshaw, Premier No.1's owner.'

Yash's lips twisted. 'You *could* say that. Please come with me.'

She led Chopra to her office and closed the door. She sat in a leather chair behind a large desk, and picked up a coffee cup. 'Dinshaw sacked me. He claimed that I was bad at my job. Hah! It was all a lie. I was the best salesperson there. Salesperson of the year, three years in a row. I asked Dinshaw for a promotion. I deserved it.

'At first he said no. And then, one day, after everyone had gone home, he called me into his office. He told me that he was thinking about my promotion. But to get it, I would need to do him a special favour.' Her lips bent into a sneer. 'You can imagine what this *special favour* was, I'm sure? Well, I refused. I had *earned* my promotion. Through hard work and talent.' Her eyes blazed with anger. 'This country was built on the backs of women. And yet equality, true equality, is as far away today as it ever was.'

She sipped loudly at her coffee.

Ganesha watched her with round eyes. He seemed very impressed by the tough business-woman.

'I told him I would go to his wife if he didn't give me the promotion. Tell her about him. But he called my bluff. He fired me, and told everyone that I had made advances towards *him*. Can you believe the nerve of the man? I tell you, I was so mad I could have broken his legs.'

She gave Chopra a hard look. 'You say someone has stolen a car from him? That he's in trouble? Well, Chopra, I couldn't be happier. I feel like shouting it from the rooftops. But the truth is I had nothing to do with it. I'm too busy to worry about revenge. When Dinshaw fired me, I didn't sit around feeling sorry for myself. I went to the bank and got a loan. Then I opened this estate agency. In three months we have become the hottest agency in the suburbs. One day, I'll be so rich I'll buy out Dinshaw. And then I'll kick him out on his sorry butt.'

Was the woman lying?

Chopra couldn't tell. She certainly had a strong motive for wishing to harm Premier No.1 and its sleazy owner. But that didn't mean she had stolen the Mercedes.

And even if she had, how in the hell had she pulled off the impossible crime?

The chef lends a hand

Chopra was puzzled. He had no idea where to go looking next.

He decided to return to his restaurant. There wasn't much else to be done. Besides, both he and Ganesha were hungry.

The restaurant was packed with people eating lunch.

Spicy smells drifted from the kitchen. Chef Lucknowwallah was hard at work preparing the delicious dishes he had become famous for.

To his delight Chopra found that his wife Poppy had joined him for lunch. She worked at a nearby school, but had taken time out to meet him. They had been married for twenty-four years, and had gone through many ups and downs together. They had even got over their sadness at not being able to have children.

In fact, this had only brought them closer.

Little Ganesha, and a street urchin named Irfan, had taken the place of those missing children in their hearts.

Chopra found Poppy in the yard at the back of the restaurant. She was sitting on the porch with Irfan, helping him as he read slowly from a picture book. The book was for infants – about a monkey that chased a ball around – even though Irfan was much older. Poppy had made it her mission to teach Irfan to read, though he made it quite a struggle for her. Irfan had lived most of his life on the streets. He had survived on his wits until Chopra had taken him on at the restaurant. (The boy now lived there, with Ganesha. They were best friends.) Irfan's progress with reading was slow but Chopra knew that his wife was a very determined woman.

Poppy Chopra was in her early forties, pretty and strong-willed. Today she was dressed in a blue sari, her dark hair in a bun at the back of her head.

Her finger moved across the page as Irfan read the words.

Ganesha came over to watch.

He loved to turn the pages of the book with his trunk. A waiter arrived with a bucket of milk for him. The milk had melted Dairy Milk chocolate in it. The little elephant was addicted to it.

'How is your day going?' asked Poppy. Chopra sat down in a chair on the porch and ordered lunch.

He told her about the case he was working on. 'Frankly, I'm not sure where to look next. And the clock is ticking.'

'From what you tell me, this Dinshaw deserves what he gets.' Poppy had very strong views on men like Dinshaw. She believed in what she called the Modern Indian Woman. No doubt she approved of Veena Yash.

'It's not just him,' said Chopra. 'The man who bought the car, Bobby Jindal, is a brutal criminal. Jon Carter, the man who hired me, won't be spared either. Others at the garage could also be in danger.'

'Do you have any clues to go on?'

Chopra took out the card Carter had given him. 'The thief left this behind. But it means nothing to me.'

Poppy read the riddle. '"A trickster came, and this was seen, In a cage went a parrot that was green, How amazing is what everybody said, What went in green, came out red!"' She looked up at her husband. 'I don't get it.'

'Neither do I.'

Chopra's lunch arrived. It was a spicy lamb rogan josh with freshly baked naan bread.

His mouth began to water. He hadn't realised just how hungry he was.

As he ate his meal, Chef Lucknowwallah

stepped out on to the porch. He lit a hand-rolled cigar, took a deep puff and blew a smoke ring into the air.

'What do you think, Chopra?' he asked. 'It's a new recipe. I've added peppers from Nagaland.'

'Mfff, mfff, mfff,' mumbled Chopra, his mouth full.

The chef grinned. Then he spotted the card on the table. 'I didn't know you were a fan of Khusrow,' he said.

Chopra swallowed, then said, 'What?'

The chef waved his cigar at the card. 'Amir Khusrow. He was a royal poet from the fourteenth century. A Sufi mystic, they say.'

'Are you sure?'

'Of course,' said the chef. 'Khusrow was born in Uttar Pradesh, my home state. Every child there learns about him in school.'

'What does the riddle mean?'

'That's easy. It's one of his most famous ones. The answer is "betel nut". See, the *green* betel nut leaf goes into your mouth, but after chewing it you spit out *red* fluid.'

Chopra thought about this. Why would a car thief leave behind a riddle from an old Sufi poet? A riddle about betel nut leaves . . .? And then it came to him. Something he had heard a few years back. It had even been in the newspapers. A car thief who had become famous for leaving behind poems and riddles as his calling card. A one-man plague on luxury cars in the city. The thief had finally been caught when he crashed a stolen Porsche into a statue of Gandhi. He had been arrested on the spot.

But Chopra couldn't remember the man's name.

He wondered if he should call one of his old friends on the police force. And then he recalled that there were a lot of policemen in the restaurant at that very moment. Once again he was glad that his former colleagues had made Poppy's a home away from home.

He picked up the card and walked back through the kitchen and out on to the restaurant floor. He called for silence, then asked if anyone remembered a car thief who liked to leave riddles at the scenes of his crimes.

'You're talking about "The Mystic",' said Inspector Rai, from the local Marol office. 'A cop I know arrested him three years ago. Made quite a name for himself.'

'What was his name? The thief, I mean.'

'I don't know. But I can call my friend for you, if you wish.'

Chopra waited while Rai made the call. Rai scribbled details on a napkin. 'The man you're looking for is Preet Hooda,' he said. 'He's out of jail now.' He handed Chopra the napkin. 'And that's where you can find him.'

The face of modern India

The road from Mumbai to the town of Pune was badly maintained. It was scarred and pitted, like most roads in India.

It took Chopra three hours to get to the Mercedes-Benz factory in Chakan. By that time he was in a seriously bad mood. The road had jarred his bones almost out of his skin, and he had been deafened by the noise of constant horns.

The hi-tech Mercedes car plant had opened some years ago, after the German company had invested fifty million dollars. The plant now made thousands of cars, trucks and buses every year.

Chopra parked in front of a swanky glass and steel building that looked like a piece of modern sculpture.

Ganesha followed him into the lobby. The space was so big it reminded Chopra of an airport. A herd of elephants would have got lost inside.

He explained to the secretaries behind the

counter that he was here to see a Mr Preet Hooda. They fussed over Ganesha while one of them made a call. She then led them out of the building and towards the main factory. They passed through a parking lot where fleets of brand new cars were parked in neat rows.

The secretary handed them over to a foreman. He told Chopra that Hooda was on the factory floor.

The foreman led them through the factory.

Chopra was amazed by it. Everything was spotless, brightly lit, and gleamed as if they were on the set of a science fiction movie. All the workers wore smart blue uniforms and caps. Some wore masks and gloves, so that not even a speck of dirt was passed on to the cars. The frames of cars moved along the assembly line, along tracks in the floor or hanging from giant yellow claws.

Chopra had never seen anything like it.

In the old India, this sort of place was unthinkable. The days of dirty, smoky factories seemed to be in the past.

This was the new India, this shiny, robotic place. A place with no soul, thought Chopra, sadly.

Ganesha, however, was utterly taken with it.

He padded along, round-eyed. The staff gave

him curious glances and smiles as he followed his grim-faced guardian. Chopra sometimes forgot that Ganesha was a child, and had a healthy sense of fun and adventure.

In this, elephants were very much like human children.

They found Hooda at the far end of the line.

Chopra explained why he was there. The former car thief, Hooda, stared at him, then asked him to come to his office.

Chopra left Ganesha behind on the factory floor.

When they were inside his office, Hooda sat down behind a desk and lit a cigarette. 'I'm not supposed to smoke,' he said, 'but what's the point of living if you can't break a few rules?' He tapped ash into a silver ashtray. 'I suppose you're wondering what I'm doing here? A car thief, working in a car plant?'

'The thought had crossed my mind,' said Chopra.

'It's part of a government programme. To help reformed prisoners to get jobs and go straight. They work with big companies to find jobs for people like me. Well, guess what? It turns out that my skill at stealing cars is worth quite a lot – to the car industry. Mercedes learned about me through the government programme. They decided to offer me a job. As a consultant helping to improve the security of their newest cars. I suppose, when you think about it, it makes sense. No one knows more about the weaknesses in cars than I do. Would you believe me if I told you I could get into your car in less time than it takes you to count the tyres?'

Chopra frowned at Hooda's boastful tone. 'So you really were the car thief known as The Mystic?'

'Hah!' smiled Hooda. 'That was the name the press gave me. Between you and me, I never did like it very much.'

'But then why did you leave poems and riddles at the scenes of your crimes?'

Hooda shrugged. 'Back then I was a younger man. I wanted to make a name for myself. I was full of pride. I knew I was the best car thief in the business. I could steal a car almost while you were driving it. I wanted the whole world to know about me, how good I was. And I loved making cops like you look stupid – no offence.' Hooda grinned, his thin moustache curling around his upper lip. 'Besides, I am a great fan of Khusrow.'

Chopra took out the black card from Premier No.1. 'Is this one of yours?'

Hooda looked at the card. 'No.'

Chopra frowned. 'Are you saying you had nothing to do with the theft of the Mercedes?'

'You can compare that card to the ones the police have from my trial. You'll see that the handwriting won't match.'

Chopra thought about this. 'Where were you yesterday evening?'

'At the cinema. In Pune. With my wife and child – and about two hundred other people.' Hooda sighed. 'Look, Chopra, I am afraid you have come out here for nothing. I have left that life behind. I have a good job, a home, a family. They mean more to me than anything. I would never do anything to risk their happiness. Besides, my time in prison has made me see the light. The state of our jails, hah! You wouldn't put a dog in those cells. Even the rats complained! And the guards? Most of them would have to *reform* just to get on the list of most wanted criminals.'

Hooda stamped his cigarette out angrily. 'I grew up in a slum. I spent most of my life sleeping on the street, begging, doing anything to put food in my belly. As a young man, I made money cleaning cars at the Taj Palace Hotel. Every day I would see these rich idiots driving up in their swanky cars. One day, I promised myself, *I* would be the one behind the wheel.

'I never stole cars for the money. I did it because I wanted to get back at all those rich snobs who parade around like peacocks while millions starve under their noses.'

Chopra was unsure. Hooda's passion seemed real. 'In that case, do you have any idea how the thief got the car out of the garage? I confess, I can't see how he did it.'

'That's because, like most cops, you have no imagination.'

'Are you saying you know how he did it?'

'Based on what you have told me, I have a good idea.'

Chopra leaned forward. 'Then tell me!'

Hooda shook his head. 'I'm afraid I can't do that.'

'Why not?'

'Honour among thieves, Chopra.'

'But-but . . . you're working as a car *security* advisor!'

'That's different,' said Hooda. 'These cars haven't been stolen yet. If I told you how your thief pulled off his trick, I would be like a magician revealing another magician's secret. It's just not done.'

Chopra had another go. 'All right then, at

least tell me where you would get rid of a stolen car like this? I mean, who could buy a car this valuable?'

'That's an easy one,' said Hooda. 'There are only a handful of men in India who could and would buy that car. My main suspect would be Manish "Manny" Singh. He runs the biggest gang of car thieves in India. He gets them to steal the best cars around. He smuggles them out of the country, sells them to African states such as Uganda and Kenya. There is a big demand for luxury cars in those places and they don't care about the paperwork.'

'Why do you think Singh would buy this car?'

'Well, for one, he's based in Mumbai. Second, he's a risk taker, like me. He loves a challenge, stealing the cars no one else would even dare look at.' Hooda grinned. 'Besides, do you know what his nickname is? They call him Mr Mercedes.'

An elephant at a car show

Chopra drove back to Mumbai.

The trip to see the car thief, Preet Hooda, had not been wasted. He now had a lead.

Manny Singh a.k.a Mr Mercedes.

The Mr Big of car theft.

After the meeting with Hooda, Chopra had made some calls to old friends on the force. He had found out that Singh was based in Mumbai, where he lived a lavish lifestyle. Like Hooda, Singh was a showman and liked to flaunt his success.

He also liked to make fun of the cops chasing him. Somehow he had avoided arrest for years.

One day, Chopra knew, the law would catch up, but until then, Singh was making merry hell.

Hooda had told Chopra that there was only one place in the country that Singh would be later that day. Singh never missed the All India Auto Show, which took place in Mumbai every year. Hooda had been planning to go, but had changed his mind. The temptation would have been too great, like a former alcoholic going to a free bar.

Back on the factory floor Chopra had found Ganesha with a group of grinning plant workers. They were watching the little elephant as he gripped an electric socket wrench with his trunk. He then used it to drive bolts into the frame of a new car. Although clumsy, Ganesha was able to get a couple of bolts in. Each time he did that, the workers clapped loudly. Chopra saw some of them handing over cash.

Clearly, they'd been having a little bet.

It didn't surprise him that Ganesha was able to use the wrench. He'd seen elephants on the internet using bamboo sticks as tools, and even painting with brushes. There were all sorts of things Ganesha could do with his trunk that Chopra hadn't even thought possible.

Now, as they drove back to Mumbai, Ganesha looked happily at him from the back of the truck. He was eating one of the chocolate bars he loved so much.

'Well, Ganesha,' said Chopra, smiling at the little elephant, 'one thing we can be sure of. No car thief will ever steal our van. Not with you standing guard inside it!'

*

It was almost ten in the evening when Chopra finally reached the Royal Shimla Hotel at Land's End. This was where the All India Auto Show was taking place. The hotel was perched on the edge of the Arabian Sea. Clumps of people moved along the seafront. Palm trees swayed in a warm evening breeze that came from the sea. A coconut seller sold coconut water from a handcart beside the entrance.

Chopra parked his car and went inside the hotel.

He joined a queue of people at the ticket booth.

When Chopra's turn came, a bored-looking man took his money, then frowned. 'Is that elephant with you?' he asked.

'Yes,' said Chopra.

'Is he going into the show?'

'Yes.'

'Why?'

'Why what?'

'Why are you taking an elephant into the show?'

'Because he wants to see the show.'

'Oh.' The man seemed puzzled. 'In that case he has to buy a ticket.'

'He's an elephant,' said Chopra.

'Yes,' agreed the man.

'Why does an elephant need a ticket?'

'Because he wants to see the show,' said the ticket man smugly.

The two men glared at each other, neither willing to back down.

At that moment, a fat man talking loudly on a mobile phone came walking along the outside of the queue. He elbowed Chopra aside as if this was the most natural thing in the world.

Chopra shook with anger.

This sort of thing was so common that most Indians just shrugged it off.

But Chopra was not like most Indians.

He hated rudeness. He hated people who were never on time. He had no patience with people who were badly behaved.

But what he hated most was people who thought it was OK to jump the queue.

Without saying a word, he grabbed the man by the neck and hauled him to the back of the queue.

The man stared at him, his jaw hanging open, the mobile phone still glued to his ear.

A round of applause followed Chopra back to the ticket booth.

The ticket man took one look at Chopra's face, and quickly gave Ganesha a ticket. 'On the house,' he said nervously.

*

The auto show was every bit as glitzy as Chopra had imagined.

Luxury cars were on display all over the place. Pouting models posed with them. Cameramen were busy snapping away, taking pictures. A red carpet wound around the displays, and bright lights made every car gleam.

Streams of people moved among the cars, staring.

Chopra pushed his way past a gang of young people crowded around a red Ferrari. A well-known TV actor was making a speech about the car. Chopra wondered if it had occurred to him that it would take a lifetime for most Indians to earn enough to buy a Ferrari. The TV guy seemed to hear his thoughts – he began talking about paying for the Ferrari in instalments.

Yes, thought Chopra, sourly, maybe they could buy a bit at a time. Perhaps start with a wingnut. Then a side mirror.

Chopra hoped that Hooda had not been wrong. The former car thief had been certain that Manny Singh would be at the event . . .

There! Chopra spotted the man called Mr Mercedes.

A tall, dark, bearded man in a black blazer, a red silk shirt, sunglasses and a black fedora hat.

Manny Singh.

Chopra noted the two big men in black safari suits standing beside Singh. His bodyguards. Each of the guards had a truncheon hanging from his hip. They were glaring at anyone who came too close, pushing away those who dared to get in Mr Mercedes' space.

Chopra realised it would be difficult to get past the two brutes. Yet he had to talk to Singh.

He had to find out if Singh was behind the theft.

'Well, boy,' he said to himself as he rested his hand on the top of Ganesha's head, 'what do we do next?'

Almost as if he had understood him, Ganesha moved away. He carved a path through the crush of people around them.

As Chopra watched, the little elephant snuck up behind one of the guards. Deftly he plucked the truncheon out of its holster on the guard's hip.

A round of laughter went up from the crowd.

Ganesha twirled the stick around. More laughter.

The bodyguard realised what was happening. 'Hey! Give that here,' he snarled.

Ganesha backed away. 'Come here, you stupid elephant!' the man growled.

Ganesha turned and vanished into the crowd, his tail swishing behind him.

'Get back here!' bellowed the guard. He turned to his partner. 'Are you going to stand there grinning like an idiot or help?'

Chopra watched as both guards ran after Ganesha. A brief twinge of worry fluttered through him. But he felt that the little elephant would easily stay one step ahead of the two clods chasing him.

At any rate, Ganesha had given him a chance and he was not about to waste it.

He closed in on Singh. The man was looking at a grey Aston Martin DB10, the car used in the latest James Bond film. The car looked like a big cat waiting to pounce.

'Manny Singh?' said Chopra.

Singh turned to peer at him over the top of his sunglasses. 'Do I know you?'

'My name is Chopra,' said Chopra. 'I run a private detective agency. I am currently trying to find a Mercedes that went missing from the Premier No.1 garage. I'd like to talk to you about that.'

An uneasy look came over Singh's face. 'Imagine,' he said. 'Being so careless as to lose a four-million-dollar car.'

'How did you know it was worth four million dollars?'

Singh's face froze. Then he forced out a smile. 'It's a small world.' He looked at his watch, a gold Rolex so fat and heavy that Chopra was amazed the man could lift his arm. 'If you want to talk to me, you'll have to do it on the run. So many cars to see and so little time!'

He turned and slipped through the crowd to the next stand along, where a black Mercedes-Maybach S600 was on display. The car was huge, almost seven metres long. 'Ahh!' breathed Singh. 'Will you look at that! What a boat!' He climbed up on to the stage and spoke to a salesman, who opened a rear door for him.

Singh vanished into the car.

Not knowing what else to do, Chopra followed him in.

With the door closed, all sounds disappeared. The smell of soft new leather and polished wood made a heady aroma in the belly of the Maybach.

'You know, this is the safest car in the world,' said Singh, stretching out his long legs. 'Bulletproof, blast resistant, steel plating in the shell. It's the car of choice for heads of state around the world. I have just ordered two.' He grinned. 'Now, how can I help you?'

'I want to know if you had anything to do with the theft of the Mercedes at Premier No.1.'

Singh stared at Chopra. 'You're a brave man, Chopra, I'll give you that. What makes you think I had something to do with it?'

'You're the kingpin of car theft. Your nickname is Mr Mercedes. You're one of the few men in the country who would know what to do with a car like that.'

'You're right on all counts,' said Singh. 'But the truth is I wouldn't touch that car. That car belongs to the gangster Bobby Jindal. You know that, don't you?'

'Yes.'

'Well, then you also know that Jindal is a man of rare talents. And his best talent is hurting those stupid enough to upset him. I steal cars, Chopra. But I'm no gangster. Jindal scares the hell out of me. Do you know what happened to the last man who made him angry? No? Let me tell you. He had him kidnapped from his home, taken to a local building site, then buried up to his waist in cement. Buried upside down. It was two days before people walking by realised that the legs sticking out of the ground weren't some sort of statue.' Singh shook his head. 'I am afraid you're wrong if you think I'm involved.'

'If not you, then who?' said Chopra.

'I have no idea. Like I said, no one in the car

theft world would be stupid enough to steal Jindal's car. You'd have to be crazy to even think about it.'

'But the thief might still come to you,' said Chopra. 'To get rid of the car, I mean.'

'Maybe. But, if he did, I'd have to tell him I'm not interested. To Bobby Jindal, fencing his car would be as bad as stealing it.'

Chopra stared at Singh until he looked away. There was something about the man's manner that didn't match his words, something shifty.

Chopra took out his business card and gave it to Singh. 'If someone contacts you trying to get rid of that car, will you let me know? A lot of innocent people are in danger.'

Back to Poppy's

Chopra dropped Ganesha back to the restaurant.

Here he found Irfan still awake after his evening's work, waiting for his friend. As Ganesha trotted into the yard, Irfan skipped over and gave him a hug. The little elephant trumpeted happily with his trunk.

Chopra watched as they began to play football, Irfan kicking the ball to Ganesha and the elephant using his trunk to push it back. They loved the simple game and could play it for hours.

A waiter came out from the restaurant. 'Sir, would you like some food?' he asked.

'No,' said Chopra. 'I will eat at home. But can you bring something for Ganesha?'

'Yes, sir,' said the waiter. He went back into the restaurant. When he came back he was holding a big box of bananas, and a bucket of milk with melted chocolate in it.

As Chopra watched Ganesha pick up the

bananas and stuff them into his mouth, he heard a voice calling him from behind.

He turned to find the garage manager, Jon Carter, approaching with a tall, fat Indian man in tow. The Indian man glared at Chopra through round, fishy eyes. 'Have you found the car?' he asked rudely.

Chopra guessed that the man was Dinshaw, the owner of Premier No.1.

'Let's talk in my office,' he said.

He left Irfan and Ganesha to their game, and led Carter and Dinshaw to the lifts.

Once inside, he sat down in his chair and pointed to the two chairs on the far side of his desk.

'I'm sorry we had to come here, Chopra,' said Jon Carter. 'But the situation is grim. Jindal called. He wants to see the car to make sure it's perfect before he gives it to his son. I have a feeling he may have heard a rumour that it is missing. We've put him off till the morning. But if it isn't there then—'

'If it isn't there, my life isn't worth a dried lentil,' shouted Dinshaw. He was sweating heavily and kept mopping his brow with a hanky. 'What have you been doing, eh? Jon told me you were the best detective in Mumbai. What use are you if you can't even find one little car?'

Chopra did not like Dinshaw's tone. The man was clearly an arrogant fool.

Quickly, he explained everything that he had done that day. He went through all the leads he had checked out, only to find that they led nowhere.

He hated to admit that he had no more ideas, but that was the truth. He had done the best he could. It didn't matter what an idiot like Dinshaw thought. Chopra answered only to his own conscience.

And yet, as he glanced at Carter's worried face, he felt a sense of regret. His failure would be terrible for the Englishman. And even a man like Dinshaw didn't deserve what was coming to him.

'Can you think of anything else?' he asked. 'Any small detail you may have missed? About the evening before the car went missing? Or the morning when you saw it was gone?'

Carter shook his head. 'There's nothing. No one at the garage was acting funny. Nothing happened that was out of the ordinary.'

'Who was the last man out that evening?'

'The head mechanic, Felix Pinto. But he left with five others, after locking up. They all swear the car was there when the shutters came down.'

'And who opened up the next morning?'

'The assistant head mechanic. But again, there were already eight other guys there waiting for him, ready to begin their shift. They rolled the shutters up, went inside and saw that the Mercedes was gone.'

'What did they do then?'

'They called me, of course,' said Carter. 'I was on my way in anyway. I had some deliveries to make that morning.'

'Deliveries?'

'Yes. We deliver to all our customers. It's part of the service. That was a busy morning. We had to deliver a Porsche, a BMW, two motorbikes and a van. I have to deliver the Mercedes to Jindal's home tomorrow evening. Park it in his garage so that he can surprise his son with it.'

'I still don't see how the thief got the car out of the showroom,' said Dinshaw. He had slumped into one of the chairs and loosened his tie, and now looked like a beached whale gasping for air.

Chopra still had no answer to this question. The thief must have waved a magic wand, and simply made the car vanish. In a whoosh of flame, perhaps.

'And why did he leave that card?' said Carter. 'What was the point?'

'To throw us off the scent,' said Chopra. 'The

thief knew there would be an investigation. Whether it was the police, or a private detective like me, or even Jindal's own men. He wanted to send us the wrong way.'

He explained his meeting with the former car thief Preet Hooda.

'And you're sure this Hooda guy had nothing to do with it?' said Carter. 'I mean, the man's a convict, after all.'

Chopra's instincts told him that Hooda had not been lying. But Carter was right. How far could you trust a man like that? Hooda had even said that he had once taken great joy in making fools of the police.

Something occurred to him and he turned to Dinshaw. 'Aren't all your vehicles insured? Against this sort of thing?'

'Of course we have insurance,' said Dinshaw scornfully. 'Do you think that matters to a man like Bobby Jindal? What shall I say to him? So sorry for ruining your son's twenty-first birthday, but don't worry. In a year's time, when the insurance finally pays out, we'll be sure to make it up to you?' He shook his head. 'This is a man who once shot a waiter for bringing him the wrong drink. What do you think he'll do to *me*?' He gave a little shiver and sank further into his chair.

'There has to be something we can do,' said Carter.

'Yes,' said Dinshaw, getting to his feet with a sudden burst of energy. 'We must run! Flee for the hills!'

'He'd find us,' said Carter. 'You know he will. And what about our families? Do we just pluck them up and vanish?'

'If need be,' said Dinshaw, though he seemed less certain.

'Where would we go? This is my home. Has been for eleven years. I'm not leaving.'

'So you would rather wait for his thugs to turn up on your doorstep?' Dinshaw waved a hand at Chopra. 'We've wasted enough time with this useless detective. It's time to face facts. We cannot find the Mercedes. There is nothing we can say to Jindal to buy more time. Tomorrow he will discover that his car has vanished. We will be lucky if he doesn't shoot us on the spot.' Dinshaw turned to Chopra. 'Goodbye, Chopra. I would like to say it has been a pleasure, but I would be lying.'

He stormed out of the office.

'I'm sorry about him,' said Carter. 'I know you've done your best.'

'No need to apologise,' said Chopra.

'He's not perfect, but he's a good man at

49

heart. He dotes on his kids. That's what it's all about, in the end, isn't it?' said Carter sadly. 'Family. A man would do anything to keep his family safe. And when a villain like Jindal is on your tail, there aren't many safe places around.' He stuck out a hand. 'Maybe, he's right. Maybe it is time to get out of here.'

After Carter had left, Chopra found himself thinking about the visit.

He hated a case he couldn't solve. He always had done, ever since he had joined the Mumbai police force as an eager seventeen-year-old some thirty years ago. But this time it was worse than that.

This time his failure would *really* hurt his client.

And that was something Chopra found hard to accept.

When he reached home, he found that Poppy had stayed up for him again. He had been so busy of late that she had taken to waiting up and cooking for him, no matter how late it was.

Now, she hummed around the kitchen, chatting away as the warm, spicy smell of chicken jalfrezi curry spread around their home.

In his bedroom, Chopra had begun to undress, changing into his night shorts.

He emptied his pockets and, as he did so, came across the pill bottle Ganesha had found in the alley behind the Premier No.1 garage.

Chopra looked at the bottle again.

The label read: SENSIPAR CINACALCET TABLETS 30MG.

He shook the smoky brown bottle – it was half full of round white tablets.

Chopra thought about the bottle. It was probably just something someone had dropped in the alley by mistake.

But the alley was locked.

Who would be in there? Why?

He picked up his phone and called his friend Homi Contractor, the senior police medical examiner at the local hospital.

Chopra had worked with Homi for years, usually when a body from the area ended up in Homi's morgue. But Homi was also a leading heart surgeon, and the Chair of the College of Cardiac Physicians and Surgeons of Mumbai.

If anyone could tell him about the tablets, it was Homi.

'Cinacalcet?' said Homi. 'What are you doing with those, Chopra? Something wrong with your kidneys?' Chopra was not surprised to hear Homi sounding alert even at this late hour. His friend had always been an insomniac.

'No,' said Chopra. 'Is that what they are for?'

'Yes. Those tablets are normally used to treat chronic kidney failure.' Homi paused. 'They are expensive tablets. Imported from America. Normally given to patients on dialysis, usually in hospital.'

Chopra's ears pricked up. 'Which hospital?'

'Well, there are only a few in the city who could afford those tablets. Around here, the best one is Lilavati.' Homi was talking about the Lilavati hospital in Bandra.

Something chimed in Chopra's head: Bandra was also where Premier No.1 was based.

Chopra didn't believe in coincidences.

'Thank you, old friend.'

'You're welcome. Are we still going to Sachin's restaurant next week?'

Chopra was a big fan of the Indian cricket player Sachin Tendulkar, who had just opened a restaurant in the city. Homi had decided to take his old friend there for a meal.

'Wouldn't miss it,' said Chopra, as he put his trousers back on.

His mind was already racing ahead.

To the Lilavati hospital.

When Poppy finally set the meal on the table and called for her husband, he was nowhere to be found.

Hands on hips, she stared at the door.

She was used to Chopra running off at odd times as he tried to solve a case, but this was strange even for him. Vanishing like that as if he were Batman and someone had just told him a cat was stuck up a tree. 'Well,' she said, crossly, 'who's going to eat all this food then?'

A warning at the hospital

The Lilavati hospital was one of Mumbai's best private hospitals. It was a grand old building that looked like a hotel, with three wings. The hospital was the first choice of film stars, politicians and other VIPs. It had the best doctors in the city and world class facilities. Recently, foreign tourists had begun to come there looking for cheap surgery.

Though 'cheap' was a relative term, Chopra thought.

No ordinary Indian could afford to be treated at Lilavati.

For the average person in Mumbai there were the government hospitals. Often, these had no money, and badly trained staff. He had heard horror stories of people going in for minor complaints and coming out with fewer body parts than they went in with. The Indian caste system was another major problem, with lower castes sometimes being refused treatment.

For Chopra, this just summed up the problems he saw in the city that he loved.

Mumbai was known as the city of dreams.

This was where people came to make their fortunes, to become famous on the sets of Bollywood, to open small businesses in the city's slums. But Mumbai was also the place where wealth and power could corrupt the best of people. If you had the money or the influence, you could get away with a lot in Mumbai, and this had always upset Chopra.

It was almost midnight as he parked his van outside the hospital.

He followed the signs to the kidney ward.

Here he found a nurse in a pink uniform scribbling on a clipboard. The nurse's name badge said: De Souza.

'May I help you?'

'My name is Chopra. I am a detective on an important case.' He took out the tablet bottle. 'I need to know if you have patients here who are taking these tablets.'

De Souza gave Chopra a look that said: have you lost your mind?

'I am sorry, sir,' she said dryly, 'but we cannot give out such information.'

'I understand,' said Chopra, 'but this is a matter of life and death.'

Nurse De Souza looked unimpressed. 'We are in a hospital. Everything is a matter of life and death. But patient records are confidential. As I am sure you must know. Being such a hotshot detective,' she added.

Chopra ground his teeth. The woman was right. 'Is this where all the kidney patients are kept?'

'Yes. And visiting hours are now closed. Sir, I must ask you to leave.'

'I *must* see the patients in this ward.'

Nurse De Souza put down her clipboard and folded her arms. 'I am going to count to three. Then I am going to call security.'

Chopra glared at the woman, then turned and went back to the lobby. Nurse De Souza followed him out to make sure he didn't try to sneak back up.

He went into the toilet, where she couldn't follow him – though he feared she might. He took out his phone and called Jon Carter. 'Mr Carter, is there someone at Premier No.1 who has severe kidney disease?'

'What?' said Carter. 'Kidney disease? What's that got to do with anything?'

'It's just a hunch,' said Chopra. 'Humour me.'

Carter paused. 'Perhaps you had better explain.'

Chopra told him about the pill bottle he had found, and how it had led him to the Lilavati hospital.

'This will lead nowhere. You're on a wild goose chase, Chopra,' said Carter, when he had finished. 'There's no one at the garage with dicky kidneys. Don't you think we'd know about it?' He sighed. 'Go home. You've done all you can. Me and Dinshaw will just have to face the music, take what's coming. Maybe this Jindal isn't as scary as everyone says he is.'

But Chopra could tell that Carter didn't really believe it.

He ended the call.

Well, there was his last lead gone.

Shaking his head, he went to the urinal.

Having used it, he washed his hands, then went out to the lobby. He hung around for a while wondering if he should have another crack at Nurse Napoleon.

He hated the idea of failure. But Carter was right. He had done the best he could.

He could do no more.

Finally, he went back out into the car park.

The van was parked at the back, beneath a row of palm trees. Mosquitoes buzzed around Chopra's head. A stray dog slipped out from under a small car and scooted across the tarmac.

He reached the van, took out his keys – and then a burst of pain exploded at the base of his skull.

Chopra fell to the floor with a grunt. He felt a heavy hand on his neck, a knee pressed into his spine, and then a rough voice hissing in his ear, in Hindi: 'Stop looking for the Mercedes. Or you'll go missing too. For good.'

And then the weight was gone.

Chopra heard the sounds of glass being smashed, and then someone running away.

He heaved himself around, and lay there staring up at the stars.

Slowly, his vision cleared. The pain in his skull became just a dull ache. He had been hit over the head with what had felt like a rubber cosh. Hit over the head and threatened.

He staggered to his feet and leaned against the van, his head still swimming. He saw that the headlights and windscreen had been smashed in.

Making sure he got the message.

Chopra felt the back of his skull. There was no blood, but he would have a good-sized lump back there. How would he explain that to Poppy?

And then there was the van. He couldn't drive around the city with no headlights or windscreen. He had urgent business tomorrow.

The repairs couldn't wait.

He took out his phone.

Premier No.1 wasn't the only garage in town.

Jonah and the whale

If the Premier No.1 garage was the poshest in Mumbai, then Kapil Gupta's garage sat at the opposite end of the spectrum. It was a hole-in-the-wall place, crushed in between stinking buffalo sheds and a shop piled high with pots and pans.

Kapil, a tall, dark man with a wrestler's frame, who wore his hair in a gelled mullet, was an old friend of Chopra's. He – and his staff of two – wore no fancy uniforms like the mechanics at Premier No.1. But Chopra trusted them. Kapil had reworked his van so that he could drive Ganesha around in it, and he had looked after Chopra's beloved Royal Enfield 'Bullet' motorbike for years.

Or 'thunder on wheels' as he liked to call it, which had always annoyed Poppy.

Kapil usually worked late into the night. Even so, when Chopra arrived, the big mechanic was sitting tiredly on a battered stool, smoking a roll-up, with a bottle of cheap beer in his hand.

Clearly, it had been a long day.

'What's the big emergency?' he said.

'Someone attacked me,' said Chopra. 'Bashed me on the skull, then smashed up the van.'

Kapil flicked his cigarette away. 'I suppose that's what you get for snooping around in other people's business.'

Though they had been friends for a long time, Chopra had always suspected that Kapil had a shady past, one that he never talked about. He was no fan of the police, that was for sure.

Kapil got to his feet. He looked at the beaten-up van, then lit another roll-up. Chopra knew this was a sign that something expensive was about to happen.

'Normally, I would have to order the screen and parts. But, lucky for you, I'm working on another van right now. It's the same sort of size as yours. I can take what I need from that.'

'What will the owner say?' said Chopra, frowning.

Kapil grinned. 'A lot. That's why I'll have to charge you double.'

Chopra thought about this. It felt wrong to delay someone else's repair. But, then again, he needed his van.

'OK, Mother Teresa,' sighed Kapil, 'if it bothers you so much, I'll give him a call. The man's an old client of mine. He won't mind waiting a few days more. Besides, I'm going to offer him a discount. Which you can pay for.'

Chopra nodded. OK.

He sat on a stool, nursing his head. Kapil and his assistant, Andy Cabral, went to work.

His thoughts returned to the case.

Who had attacked him? Why had they warned him away? Had he somehow got too close? He thought of the master criminal, Manny Singh. Mr Mercedes. There was something about him that Chopra hadn't trusted, something odd about his denials of being involved.

And what about the ace car thief, Preet Hooda? Had he followed Chopra back from Pune, then attacked him? Perhaps his pleas of innocence had been false. After all, a leopard never really changed its spots, did it? Could the thrill of stealing the rare Mercedes have lured him back from his new life?

And then there was Veena Yash, the former employee with a grudge.

Perhaps *she* had stolen the car, or had it stolen for her. After all, it was a good bet that an inside man was involved. Why not a former inside woman? Had she sensed Chopra closing in on her and sent someone after him?

'What happened anyway?' asked Kapil, as he unscrewed the damaged mounting brackets behind the right headlight. 'What sort of case gets you bashed on the head? Not that I don't like the idea of someone trying to knock some sense into you.'

Chopra told him about the stolen Mercedes.

Kapil whistled. 'I never did like that Dinshaw. But a four-million-dollar car . . . that's really something! A man in a car like that, he'd be a king.'

'What I still can't figure out is how the thief got the car out of the garage,' said Chopra.

'Perhaps it was a miracle,' said Kapil, turning the brackets over in his massive hands. 'Perhaps your thief's a genie and just rubbed his magic lamp. Or maybe he opened his mouth and swallowed it up. Walked right out with it in his big fat belly.'

'As Jonah was swallowed by the whale,' said Andy, pushing a handcart into the workshop. A windscreen was strapped to the handcart with a length of old rope.

'What?' said Chopra.

'Swallowed whole,' repeated Andy. 'Like Jonah. "And the Lord caused a great fish to swallow up Jonah; and Jonah was alive within the fish for three days and three nights."'

'What is it with you and the sermons?' said Kapil.

Chopra knew that Andy was a devout Catholic. The Catholics of India were a very committed bunch. They were the legacy of Portuguese missionaries who had arrived in the 1500s. Andy was deeply religious, and had a habit of quoting from the Bible.

'Swallowed whole,' echoed Chopra, shaking his head. Whatever the thief had done, it was a good bet he hadn't swallowed the Merced—

Chopra sat bolt upright.

Swallowed whole. From out of the mouths of mechanics.

He leapt up and clapped Andy on the back. 'Andy, you are a genius!' he exclaimed.

'"Blessed are those who find wisdom, for they shall bathe in the light of the Lord,"' muttered Andy.

'Hah!' said Kapil. 'If *he's* a genius then I must be the smartest man on Earth. What's the big deal anyway?'

'I think I know how our thief got the Mercedes out of the garage,' said Chopra.

He took out his phone. It rang for a long time before Homi came on the other end. 'It's late, Chopra. I hope this is urgent.'

'It is,' said Chopra. 'I need the complete list

of patients taking Cinacalcet at the Lilavati hospital.'

'Is that all?' said Homi. 'Perhaps I could arrange world peace at the same time? Or a trip to the moon?'

'It's important.'

'So you already said. But it's not that easy. I can't just ask for a list of patients.'

'Why not?' said Chopra. 'I thought you were the Chair of the College of Cardiac Physicians and Surgeons of Mumbai.'

A silence drifted down the phone. 'You've got me there,' said Homi. 'Sometimes I forget how much power I have . . . OK. Give me twenty minutes. I'll have to wake the top man. And then he'll have to call someone. And so on and so forth.'

Tracking a stolen car

When Chopra arrived at the Premier No.1 garage it was almost two a.m.

He parked his van, then let Ganesha out of the back. He had picked up the elephant from the restaurant. For some reason he always felt safer with Ganesha around.

After all, the little elephant had proved himself time and time again.

Chopra walked towards the front gates, Ganesha close behind. Six guards quickly snapped to attention. So, he thought, Dinshaw had doubled the guards.

The only problem was, the horse had already bolted.

He waited near the gates until a rickshaw pulled up beside him. He watched as the head mechanic, Felix Pinto, got out of the rickshaw. Felix looked at him with a raised eyebrow. 'Well, you don't expect me to pay for this, do you? I'm a gambling junkie. I'm flat broke. And thanks to you I'll probably get the sack too.'

Chopra paid the rickshaw driver.

'OK,' said Felix, watching the rickshaw putter away. 'I'm here. Now what?'

'Let's go inside,' said Chopra.

The lights came on inside the garage. Rows and rows of cars gleamed in the silence.

Chopra turned to Felix. 'When a car is ready to be sent to its client, is it logged out of the garage?'

'Of course,' said Felix. 'What do you think we are, drive-by-night merchants?'

'How?'

'Well, it's all on the computer these days.'

'Show me.'

Grumbling, Felix led Chopra to the admin office. He sat down behind a tidy desk with in and out trays and a computer.

He switched on the computer, then frowned. 'Damn. It's got a password.'

'Whose computer is it?'

Felix looked embarrassed. 'Maria's. Our accountant.'

'The one you're having an affair with?'

'The one I *was* having an affair with,' said Felix glumly. 'After you busted us in front of the boss, she phoned me up. Called me all sorts of things. I don't think she'll be letting me anywhere near her any time soon.' He shook his head. 'I really liked her.'

'Is that why you tried to get her to steal funds?'

Felix gave Chopra a sharp look. 'That was the gambler in me. And I was only going to *borrow* the money. I'd have put it all back. I wouldn't have got Maria into trouble. She's a good person, warm and friendly, once you get to know her. My wife, on the other hand, is about as much fun as an undertaker.'

'Maybe she's just fed up with you,' said Chopra. 'Can't be easy living with a gambling addict.'

'What are you, a marriage counsellor?' snapped Felix. 'No one's perfect. We all make mistakes in life. I'm paying for mine. I've gambled away nearly everything I've ever had, and now I'm about to lose what little I've got left. But here I am anyway, trying to help you.'

Chopra thought about this.

What Felix had said was true.

People were rarely simple. Good men sometimes did bad things, and bad men often did good things too. There were grey areas in everything.

Except justice.

When it came to justice, Chopra felt, there was no black and white.

He watched as Felix took out his phone and called Maria Nova. A loud voice began shouting at the other end. Felix winced.

Behind them Ganesha tapped his trunk on the computer's keyboard. His curiosity was aroused by the glowing screen. When nothing happened, he lost interest and went off to investigate the office's bin. He found a ball of crumpled paper inside, which he took out and began playing with.

It took a long time for Felix to convince Maria to help, but finally he had the password.

Once he had the right file on the screen, Chopra looked at the list of cars that had gone out of the garage on the morning after the Mercedes had vanished.

'That one,' he said, pointing at one of the vehicles on the screen.

'That?' said Felix. 'What about it?'

'It says here it was sent to a Mr Hashmi at Indus Security Limited.'

'Yes. So what?'

'I want you to call Hashmi and ask him if he received the vehicle and checked it out.'

Felix made the call.

Chopra listened in as a sleepy Hashmi

confirmed that he had indeed received the vehicle in question and checked it over.

Everything had been in order.

'OK. Are you going to tell me what this is about?' said Felix.

'Did that vehicle have a tracker inside it?' asked Chopra.

'Of course,' said Felix. 'That type of vehicle always does.'

'A GPS tracker?'

'Yes.'

'Do you have the GPS log for the journey it made from here to its delivery point?'

Felix nodded. 'We have to test the tracker out, so the first few trips are logged with us on our tracking software. Once we hand the vehicle over to the client we stop tracking it.'

'I want the data for the journey it made from here to Hashmi.'

Felix sighed. 'You know this means I'll have to call Maria again.'

He made the call. Chopra almost felt sorry for the man.

Finally, with Maria's help, Felix logged on to the GPS tracking software. He found the data file that Chopra was looking for.

Then they traced the route the vehicle had taken on that morning.

'That's strange,' said Felix, looking at the screen. 'It stopped for fifteen minutes on the way.'

'No,' said Chopra, with a look of triumph. 'That's not strange, at all. That's exactly what I was looking for.'

Abracadabra

When the owner of the garage, Dinshaw, and its manager, Jon Carter, arrived they found Felix Pinto and Chopra waiting for them in the van, along with Ganesha, padding around nervously in the back.

'I hope this is important,' said Dinshaw. 'I was in the middle of packing. I've only got a few hours left to get out of town.'

'I don't think you'll have to,' said Chopra.

Dinshaw frowned at him. 'Why? Have you managed to convince Jindal not to feed me to his dogs? I don't think so.'

'No,' said Chopra. 'I have gone one better. Please follow me.'

He drove the van away from the garage, heading towards the western half of Bandra.

Even at this time of night the streets were still busy. This was Mumbai, after all, the city that not only never slept, but also kept all the neighbours awake by playing loud music all night.

The van whizzed through the darkened roads, past the houses of the rich and the hovels of the poor, past swaying palm trees and roadside rubbish dumps. This was the time when the city was truly itself, Chopra had always thought. In the daytime, it seemed that all twenty million people were on the streets together. You could hardly hear yourself think. You certainly could not hear what the city was trying to tell you. You could not hear the city's heartbeat.

And Chopra was convinced the city had one.

Every city had one.

Since the day he had first set foot in it he had known that Mumbai was the greatest city in India. The most crowded, the richest, the most glamorous. She was also the smelliest, the noisiest and the most polluted.

Mumbai had a thousand and one problems.

And yet he loved this city. He loved how it took you in, made you a part of her twenty-million-strong family. It was not an easy city to love, especially if you were at the bottom of the pecking order. But he knew that, if you gave Mumbai your heart, then she would love you back – and that had to be worth something.

Finally, Chopra turned the van down a narrow alley full of shuttered lock-ups. He checked the print-out he had taken from Premier No.1, and then parked halfway along the deserted alley.

He waited as Jon Carter and Dinshaw parked behind him.

Chopra and Felix got out of the van. Then he let Ganesha out.

The little elephant raised his trunk and sniffed the night air, then padded around behind Chopra. He was feeling nervous.

What were they doing here so late at night?

Well, he had learned to trust his guardian, and Chopra had never let him down yet.

Chopra waited as Carter and Dinshaw approached.

'What are we doing here?' said Carter.

'And why is *that* idiot here?' said Dinshaw, looking at Felix.

Felix shifted from foot to foot as his bosses glared at him.

'You asked me to find the Mercedes,' said Chopra.

Dinshaw looked around. 'Chopra, have you lost the plot? There's nothing here. Besides, who would leave a four-million-dollar car in a place like this?'

'The person who stole it,' said Chopra calmly.

'You *know* who took the vehicle?' Dinshaw sneered.

74

'Yes.'

Dinshaw waited. 'Well, are you going to tell me or do I have to read your mind?'

'Don't you want to know how they got it out of your locked and guarded garage first?'

'Yes. I do. That must have been some trick.'

'It was a trick, but there was no magic involved. You see, the thief never stole the Mercedes in the first place. Not that evening, at any rate.'

Dinshaw's mouth hung open. 'What? What are you talking about?'

'Let me explain . . . On the evening the Mercedes went missing, the thief entered the garage from the back—' began Chopra.

'Impossible,' interrupted Dinshaw. 'There is a gated alley behind the garage. And the garage's rear door was locked.'

'Yes,' said Chopra. 'But the thief had keys to both the alley gate and the rear door.'

'Are you saying he stole the keys?' said Dinshaw.

'No,' said Chopra. 'He didn't need to. He had the keys all along. Using them, our thief entered the garage from the rear. The guards at the main gate had no clue that he was in there, because of the shutters at the front. Once inside he went to the Mercedes. He switched it on, and drove it into the back of one of the armoured vans parked in the row behind it. Premier No.1 have been upgrading them for a local private security firm. The 1954 Mercedes-Benz racing car has a single bucket seat. It is a very small car. It easily fitted inside the large van. This van was due to be sent out the next morning. Our thief knew this.

'Lastly, the thief left behind the card with the poem on it – to throw everyone off the scent. And then he left the same way he had come, through the back door. However, he made one mistake.'

Chopra took out the pill bottle and held it up.

'In his rush, he dropped this. Maybe he was in a hurry and tripped up as he was leaving, and it fell out of his pocket. Or maybe he took a hanky out of his pocket and it fell out then. It doesn't matter.'

'The thief is ill?' said Dinshaw, looking confused.

'No,' said Chopra. 'Not the thief. The thief's nine-year-old daughter. Her kidneys are failing. She needs a transplant. Soon. A transplant in India costs a fortune. A fortune that our thief doesn't have.'

'So he stole the Mercedes to fund his medical bills?' said Dinshaw.

'Yes,' said Chopra. 'The morning after he had hidden the Mercedes inside the van, he came back to the garage. This time he came in through the front door. An hour after arriving, while everyone was still in a panic about the missing car, he drove back out with the van. He delivered it to Indus Security, the client. But, on the way there, he stopped. For fifteen minutes. Just long enough to unload the Mercedes and hide it away. Here, in this alley.'

Chopra pointed at the lock-up behind them. 'My guess is that it is in there.'

Dinshaw was staring at Chopra's face. Chopra saw that the real meaning of what he had said was hitting home.

Dinshaw turned to Carter. 'But Jon, *you're* the one who made that delivery . . . and didn't you tell me that your daughter has been sick for a while with kidney problems . . .?' His voice trailed away.

Jon Carter said nothing for a while.

A dog yapped in the distance. A truck back-fired. Finally, Jon spoke: 'There comes a time when a man realises that his own life doesn't matter. All that matters is the well-being of the people he loves. His family. His children.' He paused. 'Kavita is my only child. I came to India eleven years ago, a man down on his luck. I had just served a three-year jail term. You see, I used to be a car thief. A good one. That was why I knew so much about cars. That was the reason you hired me. Of course, my references were all forged. The person your HR man spoke to back in England when he checked them out was an old friend of mine.

'At any rate, I came to India to go straight. I wanted to turn my life around. And that's exactly what I did. I worked hard, harder than I'd ever worked before. And it felt good. For the first time in my life someone gave me a chance to show what I could do. I helped make Premier No.1 the best dealership in the country. And I was honest. I never stole a penny from you.

'I met my wife the first year I was here. An Indian woman. A good woman. She's the reason I've stayed on the straight path. We married and had our daughter. I was happier than I've ever been . . . And then, three years ago, our daughter became ill. The doctors told us she had acute renal disease. Her kidneys were failing. I watched my gorgeous, lively girl become a sick child, a full-time patient, always in and out of hospital. I saw the life drain out of her. And then, the final blow.

'About a month ago the doctors told us that

if she doesn't get a transplant soon, she's going to die. But, as Chopra said, a transplant here costs a fortune. And the years of treatment, the private hospitals, have drained my savings. There was no way we could raise that sort of money. I couldn't beg it or borrow it. So the only option left was for me to steal it.'

Carter walked to the rusted shutter, took a key from his pocket and undid the padlocks. With a grunt, he rolled up the shutter, peeling paint falling on to his shoulders.

Dinshaw gasped.

Inside the cramped lock-up was the missing Mercedes.

'My plan was to get rid of it in a few weeks when the fuss was over,' said Carter.

'But by then Bobby Jindal would have caught up with us both!' said Dinshaw.

'I'm sorry about that,' said Carter. 'I didn't want to put your neck in the noose. But I had no choice. My daughter comes first. And I'm not scared of a man like Jindal. I've dealt with worse villains during my time in prison. It was a risk I had to take. No matter what Jindal does to me, if I can get the money for my daughter's surgery, I'll die a happy man.'

'Who were you planning to sell the car to?' asked Chopra.

'Manny Singh,' said Carter. 'I tried the idea out on him. He agreed.'

'You made a deal with the devil?' said Dinshaw, aghast.

'A deal with Mr Mercedes,' said Carter. 'He's the only man in Mumbai who has the guts and cash to buy that car. He's always hated Jindal. A few years ago Jindal roughed him up for stealing cars off his patch. Well, this was his chance for revenge.'

Chopra nodded to himself. His instincts had been right about Singh. He had always felt that there was something Mr Mercedes was holding back. 'So Singh helped you steal the car?'

'No,' said Carter. 'That was all my own work. He just agreed to buy it – if I could deliver it to him without Jindal finding out that he was the buyer. He didn't want to go to war with Jindal. He was happy enough to know he'd cheated him out of that car.'

Something occurred to Chopra. 'Did Singh send someone to warn me off? At the hospital?'

Carter looked sheepish. 'No. That was me. After you called me from there, I knew you were getting too close. I had to do something. I'm sorry I had to hit you. I tried my best not to hurt you too much.'

'But the man who attacked me spoke Hindi.'

'Yes. I was trying to put you off the scent. You see, I didn't tell you the truth when I said I couldn't understand Hindi. Right from the start, I didn't want you to think *I* could be involved. That's another reason why I left that card with the poem on it. I wrote it in Hindi because I thought it would mean no one would suspect me. The truth is that my wife made me learn the language. I hardly ever use it, except with her. It helps if the staff at the garage don't know that I can understand every word they're saying. I'm always catching them out when they're trying to get one over on me.'

A silence fell over the four men.

Finally Felix said: 'So, boss, does this mean I can keep my job?'

'Shut up!' Dinshaw and Chopra said at the same time.

Another silence.

Now that Carter was revealed as the one behind the theft, Dinshaw's anger seemed to have vanished. The two men had been friends for years. Chopra guessed the owner of Premier No.1 was not sure how to feel, just like Chopra himself.

Yes, he had found the Mercedes, and the person who had stolen it. And yet the price of

81

his success was to steal away hope from Jon Carter's dying child.

As if he had read Chopra's mind, Carter spoke: 'You know you've condemned my daughter, don't you?'

Chopra frowned.

Justice, which had always seemed so important to him, had been served. That was true. The car had been found, and Carter would pay the price for what he had done.

At least, that was how it should go.

And yet, and yet . . . Chopra thought of the little nine-year-old girl lying in a hospital bed. He thought of her skin going yellow from her failing kidneys. He thought of Carter promising her that everything would be all right.

It was easy for Chopra to think of justice in such black and white terms.

But it was not *his* child who was facing death.

Carter was a good man. Yes, he had made mistakes and had paid the price for them. Then he had come to India in search of a new life. And he had found it.

He had shed his past and forged a new future. He had only gone back to his old ways to save his daughter's life.

Could Chopra really hold him guilty for that?

He felt a tug on his arm.

He looked down.

Ganesha had wound his trunk around Chopra's wrist and was pulling on it. Chopra knew that the little elephant had probably sensed his feelings. Ever since Chopra had taken him in, Ganesha seemed to be able to read his thoughts.

'It's all right, boy,' he said. 'Don't worry. Everything will turn out fine.'

Chopra took out his phone. 'Do you have Manny Singh's phone number?' he asked Carter.

'Why?' said Carter.

'Give it to me.'

Carter opened his mouth, but then closed it again. With a puzzled look he gave Chopra the number.

Chopra smiled at him. 'Trust me,' he said.

All's well that ends well

Lunchtime at the restaurant.

Chopra was sitting on the porch, leafing through a case folder. Muffled noises came from inside the restaurant.

In the yard Ganesha was playing with young Irfan under the mango tree, knocking a football around with his trunk.

A steel lunch box was open next to Chopra.

Poppy, still cross at her husband for running out on the dinner she had made the night before, had made him bring the food with him to work. She had warned him that, if he tried to eat lunch from the restaurant, she would break his legs.

Chopra couldn't tell if she was joking or not.

The door to the yard opened and Jon Carter walked out. 'They told me you were out here,' he said.

'Have a seat,' said Chopra.

Carter sat down in a bamboo chair.

'Can I get you something to drink?'

'I wouldn't say no to a beer.'

They waited for the drinks to arrive.

Carter took a long gulp, then wiped his mouth with the back of his hand. 'OK,' he said, finally. 'I have to know.'

'Know what?' said Chopra, the glimmer of a smile on his lips.

'What you said to Manny Singh. He called me this morning. Told me he was going to pay for my daughter's transplant. Didn't want anything in return. Said he was glad to do it.' He raised an eyebrow. 'At first I thought he was having me on. But he kept saying it. *Insisting*. Wouldn't get off the phone till I'd given him all the details.'

'That's very good news,' said Chopra.

'It's more than good news. It's life-saving news. It's beyond anything I could have dreamed of. Last night, I thought I was facing jail. Worse, I thought I'd have to sit by and watch my daughter die. Today . . . today I feel like the luckiest man alive.' He leaned towards Chopra. 'What the hell did you say to him?'

Chopra smiled. It was time to put Carter out of his misery. 'I told him that if he didn't pay for your daughter's surgery I would tell Bobby Jindal that he – that is, Manny – tried to steal his son's Mercedes.'

Carter stared. 'You told him that?'

'I did.'

'But that's not true.'

'It's just about true enough,' said Chopra.

Carter leaned back again. 'I have to say, you surprise me. I didn't think that's the sort of thing you would do.'

'I suppose we've all learned a few things,' said Chopra. 'Sometimes, not everything is black and white.' He sipped on his lime juice. 'By the way, what happened with Dinshaw? After I left?'

'Oh, we drove the car back to the garage,' said Carter. 'And then he fired me.'

Chopra nodded. He had expected nothing less.

Carter waved it away. 'He had no choice. In his shoes I would have done the same thing. I hung him out to dry, after all. If you hadn't found the car, who knows what Bobby Jindal would have done?'

'So what will you do now?'

Carter shrugged. 'I expect I'll land on my feet. There's a new showroom opening in south Mumbai. With my track record, I've got a good chance of getting the top job. Besides, right or wrong, it helps to have an Englishman on the books in this game. Especially when you're trying to sell a pricey set of wheels to an Indian. A hangover from the days of the Raj, I suppose.'

Chopra smiled. There was some truth to what Carter said. The long years of the British presence in India had left a lasting mark on both countries.

'I wish you and your daughter all the best,' said Chopra.

Carter lifted his glass. 'To a fresh start.'

Chopra smiled. 'And a happy ending. Cheers!'

Acknowledgements

Like the Quick Reads books themselves, I shall keep this short and entertaining. Thank you first to Fanny Blake for suggesting me for this honour. Thank you to my agent Euan Thorneycroft at A.M. Heath, my editor Ruth Tross at Mulholland, and literacy consultant David Reynolds, for ensuring that this short Chopra adventure is just as polished as the others in the series. Thank you to Kerry Hood and Naomi Berwin, as always, for behind-the-scenes marketing. And thank you to the Reading Agency and Louise Davies for their tireless efforts on the Quick Reads programme.

About Quick Reads

Quick Reads are brilliant short new books written by bestselling writers. They are perfect for regular readers wanting a fast and satisfying read, but they are also ideal for adults who are discovering reading for pleasure for the first time.

Since Quick Reads was founded in 2006, over 4.5 million copies of more than a hundred titles have been sold or distributed. Quick Reads are available in paperback, in ebook and from your local library.

To find out more about Quick Reads titles, visit

www.readingagency.org.uk/quickreads

Quick Reads is part of The Reading Agency, the leading charity inspiring people of all ages and all backgrounds to read for pleasure and empowerment. Working with our partners, our aim is to make reading accessible to everyone. The Reading Agency is funded by the Arts Council.

www.readingagency.org.uk Tweet us **@readingagency**

The Reading Agency Ltd • Registered number: 3904882 (England & Wales) Registered charity number: 1085443 (England & Wales) Registered Office: Free Word Centre, 60 Farringdon Road, London, EC1R 3GA The Reading Agency is supported using public funding by Arts Council England.

We would like to thank all our funders and a range of private donors who believe in the value of our work.

has something for everyone

Stories to make you laugh

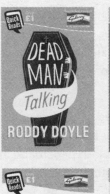

DEAD MAN Talking
RODDY DOYLE

Two women, one man...
RED FOR REVENGE
Fanny Blake

Stories to make you feel good

Looking for Captain Poldark
ROWAN COLEMAN

JOJO MOYES
Paris for ~~Two~~ One

A BABY AT THE BEACH CAFÉ
Lucy Diamond

EDITED BY
VERONICA HENRY
ANNIVERSARY
Ten tempting stories from ten bestselling authors

Stories to take you to another place

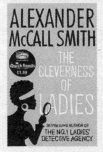

ALEXANDER McCALL SMITH
THE CLEVERNESS OF LADIES
BESTSELLING AUTHOR OF
THE NO.1 LADIES' DETECTIVE AGENCY

Jenny COLGAN
a Very Distant Shore

Stories about real life

Stories to take you to another time

Stories to make you turn the pages

For a complete list of titles visit

www.readingagency.org.uk/quickreads

Available in paperback, ebook
and from your local library

Discover the entire Baby Ganesh
Detective Agency series from
Vaseem Khan

The Unexpected
Inheritance of
Inspector Chopra

On the day he retires, Inspector Ashwin Chopra
discovers that he has inherited an elephant: an
unlikely gift that could not be more inconvenient. For
Chopra has one last case to solve . . .

But as his murder investigation leads him across
Mumbai – from its richest mansions to its murky
underworld – he quickly discovers that a baby
elephant may be exactly what an honest man needs.

Available in paperback and ebook now.

MULHOLLAND
BOOKS
HODDER

The Perplexing Theft of the Jewel in the Crown

For centuries the Koh-i-Noor diamond has set man against man and king against king. Now part of the British Crown Jewels, the priceless gem is a prize that many have killed to possess.

So when the Crown Jewels go on display in Mumbai, security is everyone's principal concern. And yet, on the very day Inspector Chopra visits the exhibition, the diamond is stolen from under his nose.

The heist was daring and seemingly impossible. The hunt is on for the culprits. But it soon becomes clear that only one man – and his elephant – can possibly crack this case . . .

Available in paperback and ebook now.

MULHOLLAND
BOOKS
HODDER

The Strange Disappearance of a Bollywood Star

Mumbai thrives on extravagant spectacles and larger-than-life characters.

But even in the city of dreams, there is no guarantee of a happy ending.

Rising star and incorrigible playboy Vikram Verma has disappeared, leaving his latest film in jeopardy. Hired by Verma's formidable mother to find him, Inspector Chopra and his sidekick, baby elephant Ganesha, embark on a journey deep into the world's most flamboyant movie industry.

As they uncover feuding stars, failed investments and death threats, it seems that many people have a motive for wanting Verma out of the picture.

And yet, as Chopra has long suspected, in Bollywood the truth is often stranger than fiction . . .

Available in paperback and ebook now.

MULHOLLAND
BOOKS
HODDER

Start a new chapter

The Beach Wedding

Dorothy Koomson

Will your past always catch up with you?

Tessa Dannall is excited and happy when her daughter,
Nia, arrives at their family's tropical beach
resort to get married.

Tessa is also trying to forget the last time
she went to a wedding on this beach and how
that day changed her life for ever.

But as the big day draws near, Tessa realises
she must face the deadly ghosts from her past
– or they may ruin her daughter's future.

Available in paperback, ebook and from your local library

Start a new chapter

The Great Cornish Getaway

Fern Britton

As the sun sits high in the sky over Cornwall, and the sea breeze brings a welcome relief to the residents of the seaside village of Trevay, there's a rumour going around.

Villagers Penny and Dorrie take charge when they hear there's a stranger in need of a hiding place. The fact that the stranger is a Hollywood heartthrob makes them even more keen to help. They both know what it's like to feel that you need a break from life, and they bring the village together to keep their stranger's secret. It's not long before he's helping some of the villagers find the answers to their own problems. In return, they find a place for him in their hearts.

Sometimes we all need an escape from the world, and in Trevay there's always a place for those who need it.

Available in paperback, ebook and from your local library

Start a new chapter

Six Foot Six

Kit De Waal

It's an exciting day for Timothy Flowers. It's the third of November, and it's Friday, and it's his twenty-first birthday. When Timothy walks to his usual street corner to see his favourite special bus, he meets Charlie. Charlie is a builder who is desperate for Timothy's help because Timothy is very tall, six feet six inches. Timothy has never had a job before – or no work that he's kept for more than a day. But when Timothy and Charlie have to collect money from a local thug, things don't exactly go according to plan . . .

Over the course of one day,
Timothy's life will change for ever.

Available in paperback, ebook and from your local library

Start a new chapter

Cut Off

Mark Billingham

It's the moment we all fear: losing our phone,
leaving us cut off from family and friends. But, for Louise,
losing hers in a local café takes her somewhere much darker.
After many hours of panic, Louise is relieved when someone
gets in touch offering to return the phone. From then
on she is impatient to get back to normal life.

But when they meet on the beach, Louise realises
you should be careful what you wish for ...

Available in paperback, ebook and from your local library

Start a new chapter

Clean Break

Tammy Cohen

DIVORCE CAN BE DEADLY

Kate wants a clean break from her husband Jack.
They can still be friends. She just doesn't
want to stay married to him.

But Jack doesn't want a friend. He wants a wife.
He wants Kate. And he will do anything to keep her.

Jack remembers his wedding vow:

Till death do us part

He always keeps a promise.

Available in paperback, ebook and from your local library

Why not start a reading group?

If you have enjoyed this book, why not share your next Quick Read with friends, colleagues, or neighbours?

The Reading Agency also runs **Reading Groups for Everyone** which helps you discover and share new books. Find a reading group near you, or register a group you already belong to and get free books and offers from publishers at **readinggroups.org**

There is a free toolkit with lots of ideas to help you run a Quick Reads reading group at **www.readingagency.org.uk/quickreads**

Share your experiences of your group on Twitter

🐦 @readingagency

Continuing your reading journey

As well as Quick Reads, The Reading Agency runs lots of programmes to help keep you and your family reading.

Reading Ahead invites you to pick six reads and record your reading in a diary to get a certificate **readingahead.org.uk**

World Book Night is an annual celebration of reading and books on 23 April **worldbooknight.org**

Chatterbooks children's reading groups and the **Summer Reading Challenge** inspire children to read more and share the books they love **readingagency.org.uk/children**